Sleeping Beauty

Retold by Anne Walter
Illustrated by Laura Barella

W
FRANKLIN WATTS

First published in 2009 by
Franklin Watts
338 Euston Road
London
NW1 3BH

Franklin Watts Australia
Level 17/207 Kent Street
Sydney
NSW 2000

A CIP catalogue record for this book is available from the British Library.

ISBN 978 0 7496 8539 3 (hbk)
ISBN 978 0 7496 8545 4 (pbk)

Series Editor: Melanie Palmer
Series Advisor: Dr Barrie Wade
Series Designer: Peter Scoulding

Printed in China

Franklin Watts is a division of
Hachette Children's Books,
an Hachette UK company
www.hachette.co.uk

Once there lived a queen who had a beautiful baby girl.

The proud king and queen invited all the fairies in the land to bless their daughter … all except one fairy who was very mean.

Each fairy gave the princess a gift. Then, just before the last fairy made her wish, the mean fairy burst in.

"You didn't invite me, so my gift is this curse!" she screeched. "On her sixteenth birthday, she will prick her finger on a spindle and die!"

The king and queen were scared, but the last good fairy had an idea. "I cannot break this curse, but I can change it," she said.

“If the princess pricks her finger, she will not die, but will sleep for a hundred years. Then she can be woken with a kiss.”

The princess grew up to be
a beautiful, kind girl.

The king and queen banished all the spindles in the castle. They never told their daughter about the curse.

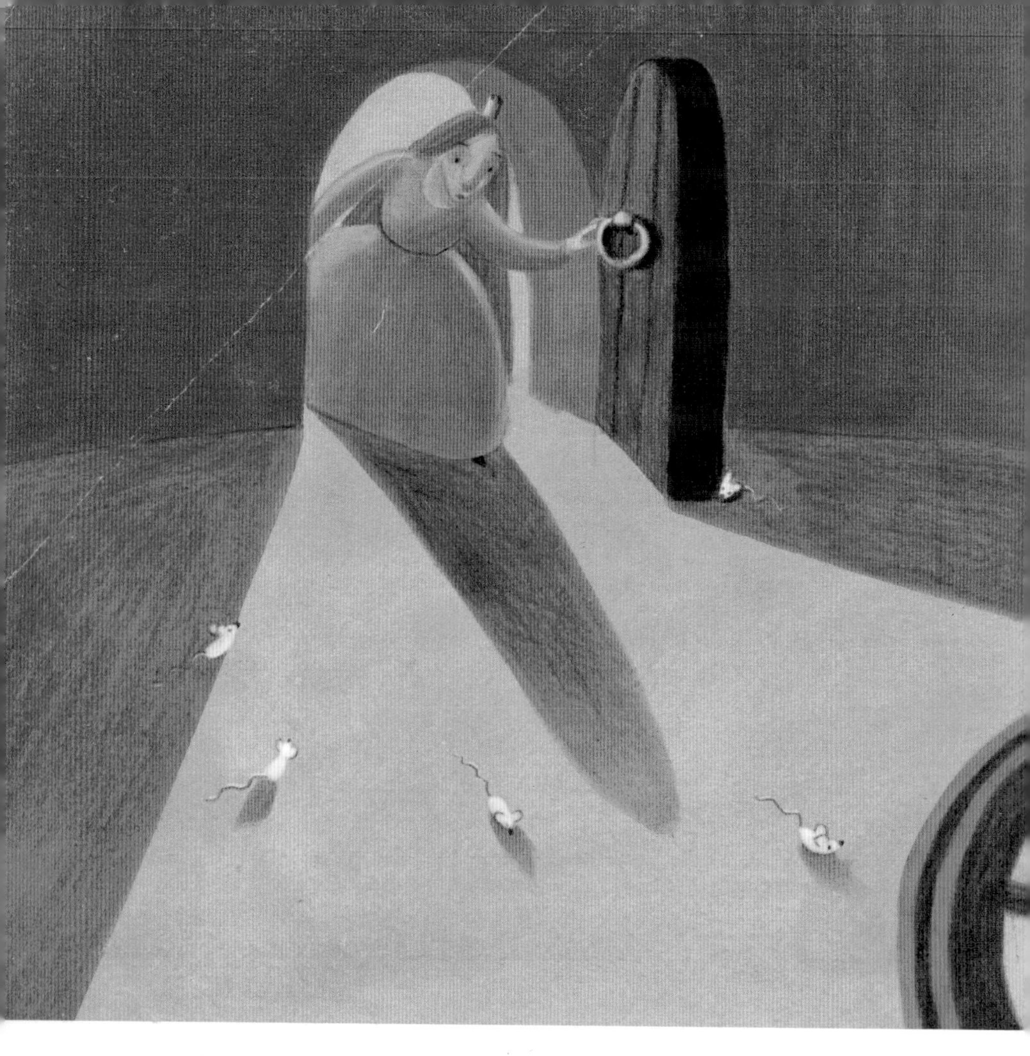

On her sixteenth birthday,
the princess found a tiny room.
Inside there was a servant sitting
at a spinning wheel.

"What are you doing?"
asked the princess.
"I'm spinning," said the servant,
who was really the mean fairy.

"Hold this!" said the mean fairy.
The princess took the spindle.
"Ouch!" she cried as she pricked
her finger!

Then she fell into a deep sleep.

When the king and queen found the princess, they were very upset. "In a hundred years, she will be all on her own," said the queen.

Then the king and queen had an idea. They asked the good fairies to put a spell on everybody.

“We will all go to sleep until the princess wakes up!” they said.

So the fairies cast their spell and the whole castle went silent as everybody fell into a deep sleep.

A hundred years passed and a thick forest grew around the castle.

Then, one day, a prince came riding by. He loved adventure and decided to explore.

Deep in the forest, he found the beautiful castle hidden in the trees.

He went inside and saw all the people fast asleep.

Soon he found the princess, still asleep. The prince had never seen anyone as beautiful. He lifted the princess's hand and kissed it. At once, she opened her eyes.

Everyone else woke up too.

The princess and the prince were soon married and the castle rang with laughter once more, as they all lived happily ever after.

Puzzle 1

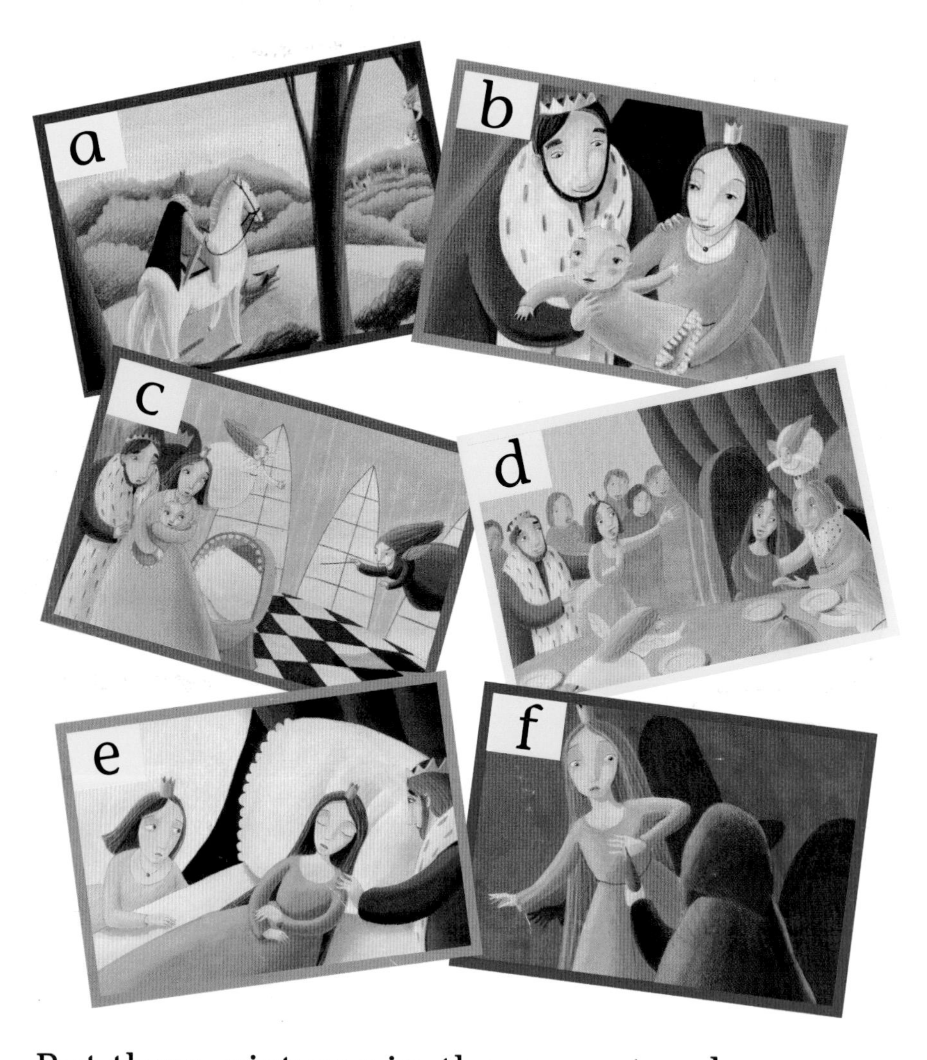

Put these pictures in the correct order.

Which event do you think is most important?

Now try writing the story in your own words!

Puzzle 2

Choose the correct speech bubbles for each character. Can you think of any others?

Turn over to find the answers.

Answers

Puzzle 1

The correct order is: 1b, 2c, 3f, 4e, 5a, 6d.

Puzzle 2

The princess: 3, 6

The prince: 4, 5

The mean fairy: 1, 2